P9-ARJ-710

THE MEADOW MOUSE
Treasury

Copyright © 1995 by Groundwood Books

All rights reserved. No part of this book may be reproduced, stored in a retrieval system or transmitted in any form, or by any means, without the prior written permission of the publisher or, in the case of photocopying or other reprographic copying, a licence from CANCOPY (Canadian Reprography Collective), Toronto, Ontario.

Groundwood Books / Douglas & McIntyre Ltd.
585 Bloor Street West
Toronto, Ontario M6G 1K5

The publisher gratefully acknowledges the assistance of the Ontario Arts Council, the Canada Council and the Ontario Ministry of Culture, Tourism and Recreation.

Canadian Cataloguing in Publication Data
Main entry under title:
The Meadow Mouse treasury

Includes index.
ISBN 0-88899-249-1
1. Children's literature, Canadian (English).*
PS8233.M43 1995   jC810.8'09282   C95-932199-3
PZ5.M43 1995

Edited by Debora Pearson
Designed by Michael Solomon
Jacket illustration by Eric Beddows
Printed and bound in Hong Kong
by Everbest Printing Co., Ltd.

PUBLISHED BY GROUNDWOOD BOOKS:

Amos's Sweater: Text copyright © 1988 by Janet Lunn; illustrations copyright © 1988 by Kim LaFave
Angel Square: Text copyright © 1984 by Brian Doyle; illustrations copyright © 1995 by Gary Clement
"The Birthday Party" from *The Charlotte Stories*: Text copyright © 1994 by Teddy Jam; illustrations copyright © 1994 by Harvey Chan
"Bounce", "The Cat Who Went Moo", "How Preposterous" and "Looking for Holes" from *Looking for Holes*: Text copyright © 1994 by Niko Scharer; illustrations copyright © 1994 by Gary Clement
"The Cycle Recycling Song" and "Mango Morning" from *Day Songs Night Songs*: Text copyright © 1993 by Robert Priest; illustrations copyright © 1993 by Keith Lee
The Dingles: Text copyright © 1985 by Helen Levchuk; illustrations copyright © 1985 by John Bianchi
Doctor Kiss Says Yes: Text copyright © 1991 by Teddy Jam; illustrations copyright © 1991 by Joanne Fitzgerald
Fall: Illustrations copyright © 1989 by Ann Blades
The Hour of the Frog: Text copyright © 1989 by Tim Wynne-Jones; illustrations copyright © 1989 by Catharine O'Neill
Morris Rumpel and the Wings of Icarus: Text copyright © 1989 by Betty Waterton; illustrations copyright © 1995 by Keith Lee
Night Cars: Text copyright © 1988 by Teddy Jam; illustrations copyright © 1988 by Eric Beddows
Pettranella: Text copyright © 1980 by Betty Waterton; illustrations copyright © 1980 by Ann Blades
Roses Sing on New Snow: Text copyright © 1991 by Paul Yee; illustrations copyright © 1991 by Harvey Chan
Very Last First Time: Text copyright © 1985 by Jan Andrews; illustrations copyright © 1985 by Ian Wallace
Zoom at Sea: Text copyright © 1983 by Tim Wynne-Jones; illustrations copyright © 1983 by Eric Beddows

PUBLISHED BY DOUGLAS & McINTYRE:

Building an Igloo: Text and photographs copyright © 1981 by Ulli Steltzer
"The Island That Took Care of Itself" from *A Great Round Wonder*: Text copyright © 1993 by Shelley Tanaka; illustrations copyright © 1993 by Debi Perna
"Times Have Changed" from *The Heat Is On*: Text copyright © 1991 by Shelley Tanaka; illustrations copyright © 1991 by Steve Beinicke

THE MEADOW MOUSE *Treasury*

STORIES ★ *POEMS* ★ *PICTURES*

FROM CANADA'S FINEST

AUTHORS AND ILLUSTRATORS

A Groundwood Book

Douglas & McIntyre / Vancouver / Toronto

LIBRARY
FRANKLIN PIERCE COLLEGE
RINDGE, NH 03461

Contents

Contents

BY ROBERT PRIEST

We had a mango morning
And everything was sun
We got out on the green grass
And we began to run

And Ishma ran like a river
And Nyima ran like a deer
Eli and I ran like the wind
And now we're standing here

We had an apple noon-time
And everything was sun
We somersaulted softly
And we sang a song for fun

And Ishma sang like a river
And Nyima sang like a sea
And Daniel and I sang Play Play Play
And all was harmony

Mango

Morning

We had an orange evening
And all the trees were sun
We slid and we were swinging
Till our mothers called us, Come!

And Jemina ran like a river
And Stevie ran like a sea
And Ananda sang like a summer's day
And all was harmony

We had a mango morning
We had an apple noon
We had an orange evening
And then we saw the moon

And Daniel slept like a tiger
And Becky slept like a stream
And Temma slept beside her
And they all began to dream

PICTURE BY KEITH LEE

By Helen Levchuk # The Dingles Pictures by John Bianchi

Doris Dingle had three cats and she loved them with all her heart. Donna, a snobby Siamese, spent most of the time sorting through her collection of bird feathers. DeeDee preferred to tap Doris Dingle's cheek with her paw until Doris opened her mouth so wide that DeeDee could count her fillings. She also liked to check up Doris Dingle's nose to see what made it whistle. Dayoh was just an all-round good guy who was digging a hole to China. When Doris called him she would yell, "*Day-oh, Day-day, Day-day, Day-oh,*" and he would come bouncing, bopping and handspringing.

Every day was a wonderful day for the Dingles. But their favorite time was breakfast. After eating they would drink catmint tea in the sunshine, then go about their business in the backyard.

One lovely day Donna was tanning her tail while Dayoh worked on his digging. DeeDee had just curled herself down into the dandelion-picking basket, when something happened!

It started out with a little breeze that blew away a few feathers. Then came a wind that tipped over a big bag of peat moss. A huge whoosh blew Doris Dingle's skirt right over her head. Doris looked up and saw a little poodle dog-paddling across the sky. Then Mr. Gonzo's union suit blew by like a big red kite with a clothesline tail—then his patio chairs and all the plastic gnomes, flamingos and whirly-gigs.

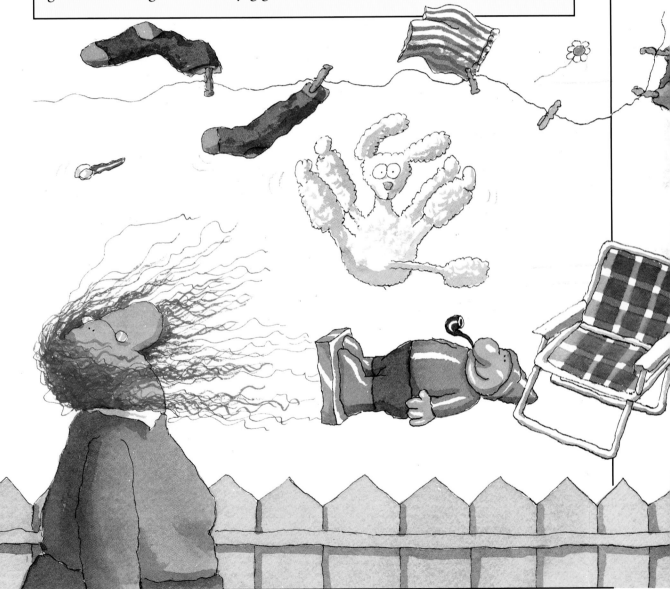

"We're going to be blown to Timbuctoo," screeched Doris, and sure enough, DeeDee came flying right by her and landed flat against the fence, spread out like a maple leaf. Then Donna and Dayoh and flowerpots, garbage pails, lawn chairs and garden hoses dumped into a big rubble pile.

But even though Doris was very scared, she made a plan. Lifting her big apron, she tore the bottom into three long strips. She tied one around each of the cats, then knotted all three to the waistband of her apron.

"Onward to the patio doors," Doris shouted, and they were off with their bellies to the ground—as flat as bearskin mats. They clung to the ground and inched toward the doors. Donna got all twisted in her cord and the others dragged her along while she said her best prayers.

The sky turned black. Rain poured down. Then, lightning struck the fence post and shot the Dingles like missiles right through the doors and into the house.

The first thing they did was have a nice bath. While the storm flashed and crashed outdoors Donna, DeeDee and Dayoh sat in a circle on the rug and had warm milk and honey with butter on top. Doris had a little catmint cordial to settle her nerves.

That night Doris, Donna, DeeDee and Dayoh crawled into Doris Dingle's feather bed. Two minutes after Doris turned out the light they were zzzzzzzzzzzzzing, as the rain pitty-patted on the roof.

Everything was just as it should be.

THE BIRTHDAY PARTY

FROM *THE CHARLOTTE STORIES* BY TEDDY JAM
PICTURES BY HARVEY CHAN

A week before Charlotte's birthday, her mother asked who she wanted to invite to the party.

"I don't want a party," Charlotte said.

"Of course you want a party. Miriam will come. And how about inviting Laura? You and Laura always play together at school."

"I don't want to invite Laura. Yesterday she wouldn't share the red paint."

"That was just a mistake," Charlotte's mother said. "How about Sarah-Jane? You have to invite Sarah-Jane. You went to her party, remember?"

"I don't like Sarah-Jane anymore. She only invited me because I said I would give her a present if she did."

"Everyone gives presents at birthday parties."

"I know that," Charlotte said.

"Nikki would be a good person to ask. You like Nikki. Remember that time he put a bandage on your knee after he kicked you?"

"Nikki smells funny," Charlotte said.

"That's a terrible thing to say. How would you like it if Nikki said you smelled funny?"

"He told me that my mouth smelled like peanut butter and I didn't like it."

"See?"

"Then I kicked him and I didn't give him a bandage. He cried."

"That was mean," Charlotte's mother said.

"I know. But it wasn't my fault. He made me."

"No one ever makes you kick them. No

wonder you don't have any friends."

"No wonder I don't want a party!" Charlotte shouted. Then she started crying and ran upstairs.

The day of Charlotte's party the sun came out for the first time in two weeks. Charlotte's mother had tied ribbons and balloons all over the house. In the morning Charlotte's father set up the barbecue and went downtown to buy special hot dogs and three kinds of ice cream.

For the party Charlotte wore her favorite pink dress with pleats on the front and a white bow that tied around her back. Before the guests came her father took her picture. "Smile," he said. "You look just like a little princess."

"I don't feel like a little princess," Charlotte said. "I hope no one comes to my party."

"Don't be silly," her father said. "You're just

feeling funny because it's your birthday. When I was a little boy I used to hate my birthday, too. One time I hid in the cupboard and pretended I was kidnapped."

"What happened?" Charlotte asked.

"No one knew I was pretending."

"I'm not going to hide in the cupboard," said Charlotte. "Yesterday in kindergarten Nikki hid in the cupboard and a spider bit him on the ear."

"You could hide somewhere else," her father said.

"I don't want to hide," Charlotte said. "You can hide if you want to. The way you did last year during my party, remember? Mommy said you hid downstairs and watched television the whole time and she had to blow up all the balloons."

"Don't be silly," Charlotte's father said. "I

would never hide on your birthday. I was just watching a very important football game. It was over by the time the other parents came."

The first guest to arrive was Sarah-Jane. She was wearing a pink dress with a white bow around its back.

"Look at you," Charlotte's father said. "You look just like a little princess."

"I know," Sarah-Jane said. She reached into her bag and took out a crown. "I am a princess."

"No you're not," Charlotte said.

"Yes I am. Your father told me and so did mine."

"Great!" Charlotte said. She went upstairs and closed the door to her room. People came and knocked on it but she called out, "Look at my sign if you can read. If you can't, I'll tell you what it says. Do Not Disturb!"

Charlotte's mother came to the door.

"It's your birthday, dear," she said. "All your friends are here."

"I know," Charlotte said. "I can see them and I can hear them and I can smell them."

"That's a terrible thing to say," Charlotte's mother said.

"That's right," said Charlotte. "I am a terrible little girl and I wish it wasn't my birthday." From her window she could see the other children

playing in the backyard. They were all shouting and laughing and playing tag with each other. Even Nikki, who was the only boy except for Patrick who was wearing his hockey sweater and Alexander who was Mary's little brother and had to come or else he would cry for a week. At least, that's what Mary's mother said. She was in the backyard, too, helping with the children and lighting the barbecue for the hot dogs.

"Is something bothering you?" Charlotte's mother asked.

"You are," Charlotte said.

"It's your birthday," Charlotte's mother said. "I don't think you're behaving very well."

"You behave," Charlotte said. "Can't you read the sign on my door?"

"Excuse me," said her mother. She came into Charlotte's room. Charlotte had changed out of her party dress and was wearing her ballet costume.

"You're a funny little girl," Charlotte's mother said.

"No I'm not."

"Is anything wrong?"

"Yes," Charlotte said. Her mother was sitting on the bed. She climbed onto her mother's lap. She closed her eyes. When she closed her eyes she saw what she had been seeing every night for a week. When she closed her eyes she saw darkness, darkness filled

with strange smells, the same darkness she had seen at the daycare when they had started playing hide-and-seek and she had shut herself in the cleaning cupboard so no one would find her.

At first it was fun and she could hear the others running around. Then the smells of the old rags made her feel sick and she was sure she could feel spiders crawling on her. She tried to get out of the cupboard but the handle was stuck. She wanted to scream but she thought everyone would laugh at her if she did because the other day Nikki had called her a crybaby when she said she was afraid of spiders.

She tried the handle again. Then she pushed the door as hard as she could.

The door flew open and she stumbled out. Nikki and Sarah-Jane were on the other side, looking at her.

"You smell funny," Nikki said.

"No she doesn't," said Sarah-Jane, but Charlotte was already running away from them, out into the playroom.

"So that's why you didn't want your birthday party," Charlotte's mother said.

Charlotte nodded. Although now, looking out the back window, she didn't mind seeing all her friends in the backyard.

When she went downstairs no one said anything about her ballet suit. Soon they all went into the kitchen and Charlotte had to close her eyes while the cake was brought in and everyone sang Happy Birthday. When she closed her eyes this time, Charlotte didn't see how it had been inside the cupboard. Instead she just felt tired, as though it was already night and she was lying in bed listening to her parents.

When it was time for her to cut the cake Nikki sat beside her. She edged away from him but he pressed his shoulder against hers and when she turned to tell him to go away he gave her such a big smile that she didn't bother.

She gave the first and the biggest piece to Sarah-Jane. The next went to Nikki. Soon everyone was eating cake and ice cream and Charlotte was listening to Nikki tell Emily that he knew how to swim and was going to go fishing with his father.

Charlotte felt happy enough to cry, but she didn't. She gave herself a second piece of cake. After all, it was her birthday party.

Looking for Holes

by Niko Scharer

picture by Gary Clement

I lost my bottom button hole
I don't know where it's gone,
It must have fallen off me
When I put my sweater on.

I was doing up my buttons
Beginning at the chin,
But the one down at the bottom
Had no hole to put it in.

I checked inside my pockets
And found a hole or two,
But not the one I'm missing
So it must have fallen through.

I found a hole for marbles
That roll across the floor,
And I found a hole for spying
In my sister's bedroom door.

I found a lot of other holes
But not the one I dropped,
I even found one like it
On my sweater, at the top!

Fall

A Picture Story by Ann Blades

AMOS'S SWEATER

AMOS was old and Amos was cold and Amos was tired of giving away all his wool. So one summer day when Aunt Hattie went out to the pasture with her big clipping shears, Amos balked.

"Baa," he cried. He butted Aunt Hattie. And ran away.

"Amos, stop!" shouted Aunt Hattie. "Stop, Amos!" But Amos did not stop. Aunt Hattie ran after him. She chased him around and around the meadow. She chased him up and down the hillside and across the brook. But Amos was too fast. Uncle Henry had to help catch him and hold him down. Then Aunt Hattie clipped his wool.

"There, now, Amos," she said. "That wasn't so bad, was it?"

"Baa," said Amos.

Aunt Hattie gave him an apple to make him feel better. But Amos did not feel better. He was old and he was cold and now he was angry.

Aunt Hattie washed the wool. She combed it and she spun it. Then she knitted it into a big, warm sweater for Uncle Henry.

"Isn't that fine, Amos?" She showed him the big, warm sweater.

"Baa." Amos snatched at the sweater with his teeth.

Every time Amos saw Uncle Henry wearing his sweater he bit it. There were always Amos holes in it that Aunt Hattie had to mend.

One hot day, when Uncle Henry left the sweater over the fence, Amos tried to pull it down. It stuck fast and he made such a huge hole in it Aunt Hattie came after him with a stick.

Aunt Hattie mended the huge hole. She washed the sweater and hung it out to dry. Amos waited for her to go back into the house. Then he made a jump for it. But the line was too high.

One night, Uncle Henry left the sweater on the table in the back kitchen of the house. The door was open. The moon was full. Amos could see the sweater from his stall in the barn.

BY **Janet Lunn**
PICTURES BY **Kim LaFave**

21

He butted the stall door. He shoved it. He butted it, he shoved it. He butted and shoved until the door flew open.

He dashed across the barnyard into the back kitchen. He yanked the sweater off the table. Furiously he pulled it this way and that. An end of yarn caught in his hoof.

He pulled and twisted to get it loose. He tugged. He twisted. He bit. He rolled around on the floor. The more he struggled the tighter the yarn wound around him. Soon he was so tangled you couldn't tell which was yarn, which was sweater, which was Amos.

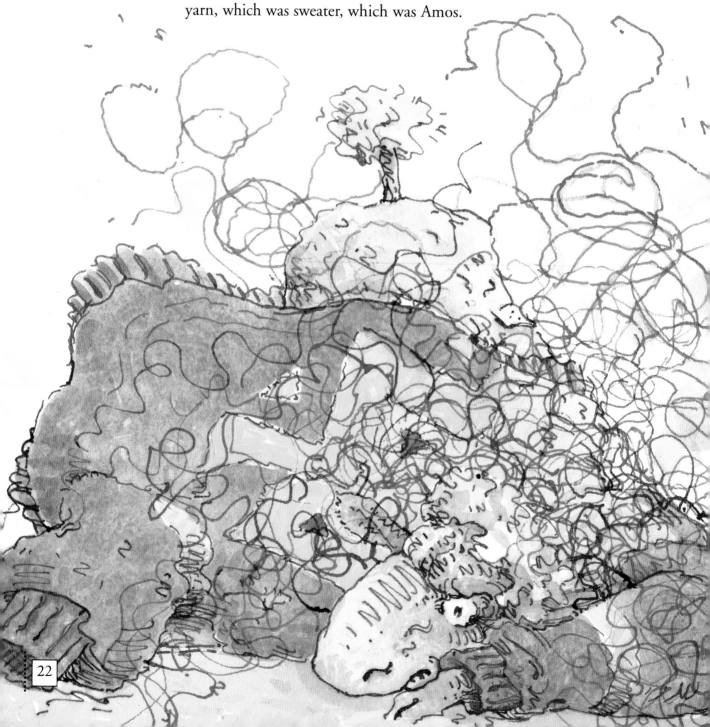

"Baa," he cried, "Baa, baaaaa," in such rage Aunt Hattie and Uncle Henry came running to see what had happened.

"Oh, Amos. Now you've done it!" Aunt Hattie sighed. Uncle Henry laughed. He began to unwind the yarn. Amos glared at them with his angry black eyes.

Free at last, he stood up. His two front legs were deep in the arms of Uncle Henry's sweater. His head poked through the top.

"You know, Hattie, Amos is old," said Uncle Henry.

"And maybe Amos is cold," said Aunt Hattie.

"And maybe," they said, both at the same time, "Amos is tired of giving away all his wool."

Now, if you go by the farm where Aunt Hattie and Uncle Henry live, you will see the sheep out in the pasture. There is one, standing a little apart. That is Amos.

He is old. But he is not cold because he is wearing his sweater.

Winter in the Northern Arctic is long and cold—so long that by September the ocean starts to freeze over, and so cold that the ice soon forms a cover two meters deep. No wonder, then, that any moisture in the air freezes right away. On cloudy days it may come down as snow; on clear days the air is full of tiny, silvery ice crystals. A new layer of white covers land and sea every day, packing down hard in some places and settling loosely in others.

Building an Igloo

Text and photographs by

Ulli Steltzer

Trees have never grown in this part of the world. For centuries the people of the Arctic, the Inuit, built their houses of snow. They called them "igloo" in some regions, "igluviak" in others. Snow was everywhere, and the only tool needed was a knife of bone, antler or walrus tusk.

Depending on the size of a family, its igloo was big or small. Even giant igloos were built as places to dance to the sound of drums. Both light and heat were provided by a stone lamp (called a kuliq) burning seal fat and using the cotton-like seeds of a small plant for a wick. Of course, each igloo needed a chimney where hot air could escape, or the whole top would begin to melt and might cave in on the people.

When many people lived in an igloo, they sometimes damaged its walls. Rather than continually patching their igloo, the family would build a new one. Often an igloo was abandoned because the family moved to better hunting grounds, leaving their old house to melt away in the summer sun.

Tookillkee Kiguktak lives in Griese Fiord, the most northern settlement in Canada, on Ellesmere Island. He does not live in an igloo; like all the Inuit of today he lives in a house. But when Tookillkee was a little child he lived in an igloo, and when he was a boy he learned how to build one. Ever since, when he goes hunting far away for a musk ox or a polar bear, he builds an igloo for shelter.

A hunter never goes alone on a long trip. Tookillkee likes to take along Jopee, one of his four sons, and of course Jopee—like his father—long ago learned how to build an igloo.

It takes several hours of hard work to build a good igloo. The most important thing is to find the right kind of snow. Not too soft, not too hard.

Tookillkee starts walking over the land. Only when the surface remains unbroken under his feet does he stop. With his carpenter saw he checks the depth and quality of the snow. On a rocky slope, like the site shown here, he has to be especially careful to find a large enough area of good snow. Once he has found it, he steps to one side of the good snow and paces off a circle. This is where he will build his igloo.

Tookillkee outlines the blocks in the snow before he cuts them. Then, with the blade of the saw, he lifts up each one. It can weigh from eight to twelve kilograms depending on size. He lines up the blocks alongside the growing trench from which they were cut.

When he has cut all the blocks, it is time to start building the igloo.

He cuts diagonally into the blocks to start a spiral.

Jopee helps with the carrying. Before bringing a fresh block, he waits until his father has set the last one in position.

After setting each block, Tookillkee trims and cleans its surface with a long knife.

The final blocks that round off the top need skillful shaping and fitting.

Tookillkee reaches up and places the last block, the keystone of the igloo. He is locked in.

With his knife he cuts a low doorway and crawls out.

After the two men fill in the cracks with

the soft snow from the undercut side of the blocks, Tookillkee builds a chimney.

Then he cuts a window in the front, above the entrance. He has chosen a piece of ice from the ocean for a window pane. It gives much light to the inside, a strange, blue-green light like that surrounding a swimmer under water.

Tookillkee decides to build a porch. It will keep the cold draft from coming inside and will give him storage space, especially for food, boots and bulky clothing. He cuts more snow blocks. After attaching the first two rows to both sides of the igloo's entrance, he rounds off the top on the gentle slope of a spiral. No chimney is needed for the porch, and the cracks are filled in quickly.

The igloo is ready.

It is evening. Father and son settle down inside. They look out on the frozen ocean. Tomorrow will be a day of hunting.

PETTRANELLA

BY Betty Waterton

PICTURES BY Ann Blades

LONG ago in a country far away lived a little girl named Pettranella. She lived with her father and mother in the upstairs of her grandmother's tall, narrow house.

Other houses just like it lined the street on both sides, and at the end of the street was the mill. All day and all night smoke rose from its great smokestacks and lay like a gray blanket over the city. It hid the sun and choked the trees, and it withered the flowers that tried to grow in the window boxes.

One dark winter night when the wind blew cold from the east, Pettranella's father came home with a letter. The family gathered around the table in the warm yellow circle of the lamp to read it; even the grandmother came from her rooms downstairs to listen.

"It's from Uncle Gus in Canada," began her father. "He has his homestead there now, and is already clearing his land. Someday it will be a large farm growing many crops of grain." And then he read the letter aloud.

When he had finished, Pettranella said, "I wish we could go there, too, and live on a homestead."

Her parents looked at each other, their eyes twinkling with a secret. "We *are* going," said her mother. "We are sailing on the very next ship."

Pettranella could hardly believe her ears. Suddenly she thought of some things she had always wanted. "Can we have some chickens?" she asked. "And a swing?"

"You will be in charge of the chickens," laughed her father, "and I will put up a swing for you in our biggest tree."

"And Grandmother," cried Pettranella, "now you will have a real flower garden, not just a window box."

Pulling her close, the grandmother said gently, "But I cannot go to the new land with you, little one. I am too old to make such a long journey."

Pettranella's eyes filled with tears. "Then I won't go either," she said.

But in the end, of course, she did. When they were ready to leave, her grandmother gave her a small muslin bag. Pettranella opened it and looked inside. "There are seeds in here!" she exclaimed.

"There is a garden in there," said the old lady. "Those are flower seeds to plant when you get to your new home."

"Oh, I will take such good care of them," promised Pettranella. "And I will plant them and make a beautiful garden for you."

So they left their homeland. It was sad, thought Pettranella, but it was exciting, too. Sad to say good-bye to everyone they knew, and exciting to be going across the ocean in a big ship.

But the winter storms were not over, and as the ship pitched about on the stormy seas everyone was seasick. For days Pettranella lay on her wooden bunk in the crowded hold, wishing she was back home in her clean, warm bed.

At last they reached the shores of Canada. Pettranella began to feel better. As they stood at the rail waiting to leave the ship, she asked, "Can we see our homestead yet?"

Not yet, they told her; there was still a long way to go.

Before they could continue their journey her father had to fill out many forms, and Pettranella spent hours and hours sitting on their round-topped trunk in a crowded building, waiting. So many people, she thought. Would there be room for them all?

Finally one day the last form was signed and they were free to go, and as they traveled up a wide river and across the lonely land, Pettranella knew that in this big country there would be room for everyone.

After many days they came to a settlement where two rivers met and there they camped while the father got his homestead papers. Then they bought some things they would need: an ax and a saw, a hammer and nails, sacks of food and seed, a plow and a cow and a strong brown ox, and a cart with two large wooden wheels. And some chickens.

The ox was hitched to the cart, which was so full of all their belongings that there was barely room for Pettranella and her mother. Her father walked beside the ox, and the cow followed.

The wooden wheels creaked over the bumpy ground, and at first Pettranella thought it was fun, but soon she began asking, "When are we going to get there?" and making rather a nuisance of herself climbing in and out of the cart.

Often at night as they lay wrapped in their warm quilts beside the fire, they heard owls hooting, and sometimes wolves calling to one another; once they saw the northern lights.

One day as they followed the winding trail through groves of spruce and poplar, there was a sudden THUMP, CRACK, CRASH!

"What happened?" cried Pettranella, as she slid off the cart into the mud.

"We have broken a shaft," said her father.

"One of the wheels went over a big rock."

"Now we'll never find our homestead!" wailed Pettranella, as they began to unload the cart. "We'll make a new shaft," said her father; and, taking his ax, he went into the woods to cut a pole the right size.

Pettranella helped her mother make lunch, then sat down on a log to wait. Taking the bag of seeds from her pocket, she poured them out into a little pile on her lap, thinking all the while of the garden she would soon be making.

Just then she heard something. A familiar creaking and squeaking, and it was getting closer. It had to be—it was—another ox cart!

"Somebody's coming!" she shouted, jumping up.

Her father came running out of the woods as the cart drew near. It was just like theirs, but the ox was black. The driver had a tanned, friendly face. When he saw their trouble, he swung down from his cart to help. He helped the father make a new shaft, then they fastened it in place and loaded the cart again.

Afterwards they all had lunch, and Pettranella sat listening while the grownups talked together. Their new friend had a homestead near theirs, he said, and he invited them to visit one day.

"Do you have any children?" asked Pettranella.

"A little girl just like you," he laughed, as he climbed into his cart. He was on his way to get some supplies. Pettranella waved good-bye as he drove off, and they set forth once again to find their homestead. "Our neighbor says it isn't far now," said her father.

As they bumped along the trail, suddenly Pettranella thought about the flower seeds. She felt in her pocket, but there was nothing there. The muslin bag was gone!

"Oh, no! Stop!" she cried. "The seeds are gone!"

Her father halted the ox. "I saw you looking at them before lunch," said her mother. "You must have spilled them there. You'll never find them now."

"I'm going back to look anyway," said Pettranella, and, before they could stop her, she was running back down the trail.

She found the log, but she didn't find any seeds. Just the empty muslin bag.

As she trudged back to the cart, her tears began to fall. "I was going to make such a beautiful garden, and now I broke my promise to Grandmother!"

"Maybe you can make a vegetable garden instead," suggested her mother, but Pettranella knew it wouldn't be the same. "I don't think turnips and cabbages are very pretty," she sighed.

It was later that afternoon, near teatime, when they found their homestead.

Their own land, as far as they could see! Pettranella was so excited that for a while she forgot all about her lost seeds.

That night they slept on beds of spruce and tamarack boughs cut from their own trees. What a good smell, thought Pettranella, snuggling under her quilt.

The next morning her father began to put up a small cabin; later he would build a larger one. Then he started to break the land. A small piece of ground was set aside for vegetables, and after it was dug, it was Pettranella's job to rake the earth and gather the stones into a pile.

"Can we plant the seeds now?" she asked when she had finished.

"Not yet," said her mother, "it's still too cold."

One morning they were awakened by a great noise that filled the sky above them. "Wild geese!" shouted the father, as they rushed outside to look. "They're on their way north. It's really spring!"

Soon squirrels chattered and red-winged blackbirds sang, a wobbly-legged calf was born to the cow, and sixteen baby chicks hatched.

"Now we can plant the garden," said the mother, and they did.

Early the next morning Pettranella ran outside to see if anything had sprouted yet. The soil was bare; but a few days later when she looked, she saw rows of tiny green shoots.

If only I hadn't lost Grandmother's seeds, she thought, flowers would be coming up now, too.

One warm Sunday a few weeks later, Pettranella put on a clean pinafore and her best sunbonnet and went to help her father hitch up the ox, for this was the day they were going to visit their neighbors.

As the ox cart bumped and bounced down the trail over which they had come so many weeks before, Pettranella thought about the little girl they were going to visit. She will probably be my very best friend, she thought to herself.

Suddenly her father stopped the cart and jumped down. "There's the rock where we broke the shaft," he said. "This time I will lead the ox around it."

"There's where we had lunch that day," said her mother.

"And there's the log I was sitting on when I lost the seeds," said Pettranella. "And look! LOOK AT ALL THOSE FLOWERS!"

There they were. Blowing gently in the breeze, their bright faces turned to the sun and their roots firm in the Canadian soil— Grandmother's flowers.

"Oh! Oh!" cried Pettranella, "I have never seen such beautiful flowers!"

Her mother's eyes were shining as she looked at them. "Just like the ones that grew in the countryside back home!" she exclaimed.

"You can plant them beside our house," said her father, "and make a flower garden there."

Pettranella did, and she tended it carefully, and so her promise to her grandmother was not broken after all.

But she left some to grow beside the trail, that other settlers might see them and not feel lonely; and to this very day, Pettranella's flowers bloom each year beside a country road in Manitoba.

Little Sue Nichol had a tricycle
But little wee Suzy grew
Till that little three-wheeler was tooo
    small
So what did big Sue do?

Recycle that tricycle
O cycle recycle it please
Recycle that tricycle
It's just what someone else needs

Great big Ike had a great big bike
But great big Ikey grew
Till that big two-wheeler was tooo small
So what did huge Ike do?

Recycle that bicycle
Trade it in for something else please
Recycle that bicycle
It's just what someone else needs

Round and round and round and
    round it goes
Not just bikes but toys and boats and
    bottles
And baby clothes

Little wee Michael had a unicycle
But little wee Michael grew
Till that little one-wheeler was tooo
    small
So what did big Mike do?

Recycle that unicycle
He sold it to some clown
Recycle that unicycle
It still goes round and round and round
    and

Round and round and round and round
    it goes
Not just trikes but books and bells and
    paper
And pianos

Now big Sue Nichol has a bi-cycle!

33

ZOOM *at* SEA

by TIM WYNNE-JONES

ZOOM loved water. Not to drink—he liked cream to drink—Zoom liked water to play with.

One night, when a leaky tap filled the kitchen sink, Zoom strapped wooden spoons to his feet with elastic bands and paddled in the water for hours. He loved it.

The next night he made a boat from a wicker basket with a towel for a sail. Blown around the bathtub all night, he was as happy as could be.

There was no stopping him. Every night when other self-respecting cats were out mousing and howling Zoom stayed indoors and sailed about in the dark. By day he watched the tap and dreamed.

One afternoon while dreaming in the attic he noticed a shelf he had not seen before. A dusty diary lay next to a photograph of a large yellow tom cat with white whiskers and a black sou'wester. It was inscribed:

"For Zoom from Uncle Roy."

Zoom opened the diary and on the last page he found an address and a map. "The Sea and how to get there," it said.

The Sea was not far, really. Zoom took a bus. He arrived very early in the morning, at a house with a big front door. It was so early Zoom was afraid to knock but the light was on and if he listened closely he thought he could hear someone inside. With great excitement he rapped three times.

The door opened. Before him stood a large woman in a blue dress. She wore silver earrings and many silver bracelets on her wrists.

"I want to go to sea," said Zoom nervously.

The woman smiled, but said nothing. Zoom spoke louder.

"I'm Uncle Roy's nephew and I want to go to sea."

"Ahh!" said the woman, nodding her head. "Come in my little sailor."

Inside was cold and damp.

"I am Maria," said the woman. "I'm not ready just yet."

pictures by ERIC BEDDOWS

The room was quiet and dark; everything was still. Far away Zoom could hear a sound like a leaky faucet.

He sat, trying to be patient, while Maria bustled around. Sometimes it was difficult to see her in the gloom, but he could hear the swish of her skirts and the tinkling of her bracelets.

The Sea was nothing like Uncle Roy had described in his diary. Zoom was sure he had made a mistake and he was just about to sneak away when Maria looked at her watch and winked.

"Now I'm ready."

And with that, she turned an enormous wheel several times to the right. The floor began to rumble and machinery began to whirr and hum. The room grew lighter and Zoom saw that it was very large.

Now Maria pushed a button and cranked a crank. Zoom could hear the sound of water rushing through the pipes. First there were only puddles but then it poured from the closets and lapped at his feet.

From rows upon rows of tiny doors Maria released sea gulls and sandpipers, pelicans and terns. From pots and cages she set free hundreds of crabs and octopi and squid who scurried this way and that across the sandy floor.

Maria laughed. Zoom laughed. This was more like it. Noise and sunlight and water, for now there was water everywhere.

Suddenly Zoom realized he could not even see the walls of this giant room. Only the sun coming up like gold, and silver fish dancing on the waves. Far away he could see a fishing boat.

Maria smiled and said, "Go on. It's all yours."

Quickly he gathered some old logs and laced them together with seaweed. He made a raft and decorated it with shells as white as Maria's teeth.

When it was ready, he pushed and he heaved with all his might and launched the raft into the waves.

"I'm at Sea!" he called.

He danced around on his driftwood deck and occasionally cupped his paws and shouted very loudly back to shore.

"More waves," or "More Sun," or "More fish."

Waves crashed against the raft. The sun beat down. Fish leaped across the bow and frolicked in his wake.

Zoom looked back towards the shore and saw Maria. He realized, then, that he was tired. The waves subsided and the water gently began to roll towards the shore. Zoom sat and let the tide drift him back.

He sat with Maria at her little table drinking tea and eating fish fritters and watched the sun sink into the sea. As the light dimmed the room didn't seem half so big.

Maria's bun had come undone and there was sand in the ruffles at the bottom of her dress, but still she smiled and her jewelry tinkled silver in the twilight.

"Thank you for a great day," said Zoom as he stood at the door. "May I come back?"

"I'm sure you will," said Maria.

And he did.

Poems by NIKO SCHARER

The Cat Who Went Moo

There once was a cat who went Moo.
She said, "Oh, what can I do?
I should go Meow
Not Moo like a cow,"
So sadly she cried, "Moo hoo."

How Preposterous

Margaret's so preposterous
She swallowed a rhinoceros!
She ate him up from tail to snout
(Except the parts she spit back out.)
She munched his toes and crunched his feet,
She spread grape jelly on the meat.
She stuffed his horn with pickled eel
And fried the wrinkles on his heel.
She dipped the bones in sour cream
And licked his knobby knuckles clean.
At last she ate his tangled hair
And then the rhino wasn't there.
How awful, how preposterous!
She ate the *whole* rhinoceros
And didn't share with me.

Bounce

I have a friend and his name is Bounce,
And he weighs a ton if he weighs an ounce.
But Bounce can bounce both up and down,
Why Bounce can bounce the best in town!

And Bounce wears boots as big as boats
And a black beret and a big black coat.
And Bounce can bounce like a rubber ball,
His bouncing's really off the wall.

He can bounce a ball, he can bounce a man,
He can bounce a flea off an old tin can.
He can bounce so high that he won't come down,
He can bounce from here to Charlottetown!

BY *Teddy Jam*

DOCTOR KISS SAYS YES

PICTURES BY *Joanne Fitzgerald*

One day after Doctor Kiss got home from school she found an envelope under her pillow. Inside the envelope were two cardboard squares and a letter.

One cardboard square was red. The other was green. Doctor Kiss read the letter and then she read it again.

"Yes!" said Doctor Kiss. She opened her doctor kit, took out some tape, and taped the green square to the window.

"Are you hungry?" asked Doctor Kiss's mother at supper.

"Yes!" said Doctor Kiss, because she knew she would have to be very strong tonight.

"Are you ready to go to your room?" asked Doctor Kiss's father when it was time for bed.

"Yes!" said Doctor Kiss, climbing onto her father's shoulders. She wanted to go to bed and get ready for her adventure.

"Do you want us to turn out your light?" asked Doctor Kiss's mother and father after they had read her a story, given her one million kisses, fifteen hugs, forty squeezes and five tickles for good luck.

Doctor Kiss's mother put on Doctor Kiss's favorite tape. Doctor Kiss's father brought Doctor Kiss one box of pineapple juice with a straw, one apple cut into eight pieces and her doctor kit.

"Goodnight Doctor Kiss," said Doctor Kiss's mother.

"Goodnight Doctor Kiss," said Doctor

Dear Doctor Kiss:

We need your help tonight.

Will you come?

X.

Kiss's father.

"Goodnight," said Doctor Kiss. "Please don't forget to close my door."

Doctor Kiss put on her clothes and climbed out the window.

At the edge of the forest a young squire was waiting for her with a horse. "Thank you for coming, Doctor Kiss. We saw your signal in the window. Would you like to ride this horse?"

"Yes!" said Doctor Kiss.

They galloped through the forest. Doctor Kiss felt the moonlight and the wind against her face. They rode until they came to a small clearing. In the middle was a tall tent.

"Here we are," said the squire.

Inside the tent, lying on cushions and blankets, was a knight. His weapons and armor were piled beside him. Kneeling and holding his hand was a beautiful lady with long hair.

"Oh Doctor Kiss!" cried the damsel. "Can you help this poor broken knight?"

"I hope so," said Doctor Kiss. "What is the matter?"

The damsel began to weep. The squire turned away because he did not want anyone to see him cry. "This afternoon there was a terrible battle. My brave knight and his friends were riding through the forest singing songs.

Then they were attacked by evil knights riding giant black horses."

"How terrible," said Doctor Kiss.

"They fought for hours, crashing their swords against each other and roaring like lions."

"What an enormous noise," said Doctor Kiss.

"Sir Roderick charged three of the black knights at once."

"How brave," said Doctor Kiss.

"Sir Gawain fought with his cat on his shoulder."

"How unusual," said Doctor Kiss.

"When Sir Gawain was knocked from his horse, my Roderick gathered up Gawain and his cat and rode them to safety."

"How gallant," said Doctor Kiss.

"Now Sir Gawain is home with his mother."

"And Roderick?"

"Here. Beneath these blankets. Growing ever weaker."

"What happened to him?" asked Doctor Kiss.

"He scraped his knees and now they are extremely sore."

Doctor Kiss leaned over the knight's knees and looked at them.

"They both hurt," declared Sir Roderick. "Mighty thumps did they receive as the giant black horses crashed against them. Once, twice,

a thousand times I was squeezed between those beasts. Can you make them better?"

"Yes!" said Doctor Kiss. She took a box out of her doctor kit and opened it up. "This is one of my secrets," she said. Then she found two big bandages and put them on his knees.

"Are they all better?"

"Yes!" said Doctor Kiss.

"But they still hurt."

"Well then," said Doctor Kiss, "count to a thousand and then go to sleep. In the morning you will be a new knight."

"I still can't sleep," said Sir Roderick. "I need one million kisses, fifteen hugs, forty squeezes and five tickles for good luck. Also, if you don't mind, one box of pineapple juice with a straw and one apple cut into eight pieces."

"All right," said Doctor Kiss.

Doctor Kiss left the tent. The moon was above her in the sky. It shone down on the knight's mysterious tent and made little moons in the eyes of the horse that was waiting to carry her home.

At breakfast Doctor Kiss's mother asked if she had slept well.

"Yes!" said Doctor Kiss.

"Are you hungry?" asked her father.

"Yes!" said Doctor Kiss. "Very."

Times have changed! Our energy needs— **Then**

We haven't always used so much energy. Only one hundred years ago, perhaps when your great-great-grandparents were growing up, life was quite different. In fact, a typical winter day might have gone something like this:

5:30 a.m. Hear early-morning sounds of father down in kitchen, throwing more wood into stove (only source of heat in house).

6:30 a.m. Get up when morning light streams through window. Your room is so cold that you can see your breath. Wooden floor feels freezing cold on your bare feet. Quickly put on several layers of clothing and go downstairs. Rush outside to outhouse to go to bathroom.

7:00 a.m. Porridge is bubbling on wood stove. Cut thick slice of bread and clamp between two wire racks. Place over open stove top to make toast. Get butter out of ice box. Fetch potatoes, squash, carrots and onions from cellar and cut up stew for dinner, which will sit cooking all day while warmth from stove heats house.

8:00 a.m. Gather up books and leave house for 45-minute walk to school.

9:00 a.m. Put container of milk in stream by school to keep cool. Help gather wood for stove that keeps schoolhouse warm.

Now

By *Shelley Tanaka*
Pictures by *Steve Beinicke*

On the other hand, a typical kid's day today would be quite different:

8:00 a.m. Wake up to sound of clock radio. Check digital clock for time, press Doze button and go back to sleep for 10 minutes.

8:15 a.m. Have hot shower. Dry hair with blow-dryer. Sort through laundry in dryer for favorite T-shirt.

8:30 a.m. Listen to weather forecast on radio Plug in kettle to boil water for instant hot chocolate. Make toast in automatic toaster. Grab Walkman and books and rush out door. Beg Mum for lift home since rain is predicted.

9:00 a.m. Arrive at school. Today's classes include computers, language lab and a film on windmills.

3:30 p.m. Mum waiting in car outside school, engine running. Drive 10 blocks home. Stop off at mall on the way; play video game while Mum does insta-banking, picks up dry-cleaning and buys hamburger buns for dinner.

4:00 p.m. Grab snack out of fridge, phone best friend for chat. Play stereo while doing homework. Turn up volume when noise of vacuum cleaner in next room gets too loud.

Then

3:30 p.m. Walk home to do chores. Sweep floors. Chop wood for stove and bring into house. Take dry clothes off line and fold or iron, using iron heated on stove.

5:00 p.m. Light oil lamps as it begins to get dark. Eat dinner while discussing chores to be done next day.

5:30 p.m. Pour hot water from pot on stove into dishpan. Wash dishes by hand and dry them with dishcloth. Cover bowl of leftover food with tea towel and place in unheated room next to kitchen to keep cool.

7:00 p.m. Do homework by light of oil lamp. Get out skates and polish so they will be ready when pond freezes over after Christmas. Do hand mending. Write letters. Fill hot-water bottle with hot water and run upstairs to put under covers to warm bed. Hurry back down to warm kitchen.

8:30 p.m. Eyes getting sore from reading in dim light. Go upstairs and quickly get into bed. Sounds drift up through hole in floor that lets heat rise up from kitchen into your room. Fall asleep to sounds of parents putting more wood into stove for the night before they go to bed, too.

Now

6:00 p.m. Go into kitchen to help prepare dinner. Defrost meat in microwave. Chop onions in food processor for hamburgers, take frozen French fries out of freezer, preheat broiler in oven, switch on automatic coffeemaker.

6:30 p.m. Eat dinner while listening to evening news on radio.

7:00 p.m. Put dishes in dishwasher. Cover leftover food with plastic wrap and put in refrigerator.

7:15 p.m. Get ride to hockey practice. Hang out with friends while Zamboni clears artificial ice. Get cold drink from pop machine.

8:30 p.m. Home from practice, watch movie on VCR. Turn up heat a bit since house seems kind of chilly.

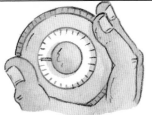

10:30 p.m. Listen to Walkman in bed before turning off light. Fall asleep listening to hum of fridge, occasional clunk of electric furnace going on, and faint noises from TV still on in living room.

from Angel Square

By Brian Doyle
Pictures by Gary Clement

Our teacher, Mr. Maynard, was telling us again about the eclipse and how the earth stands between the sun and the moon and blocks out the light. And how you can see the shadow of the earth crossing the moon until the moon is completely dark.

Mr. Maynard, for homework, told us to watch it from nine o'clock to nine-thirty. The complete eclipse would be at exactly nine-twenty.

Killer Bodnoff said he could stay up all right but he couldn't watch the eclipse because "Gangbusters" was on the radio at nine.

Arnold Levinson said he'd try to watch it but he didn't know if he could last because he gets awful tired and anyway he's afraid of the dark.

Anita Pleet could watch it, yes, and as a matter of fact she had her own telescope and she'd do a project on it for Mr. Maynard if he'd like.

Martha Banting couldn't stay up because she was too nice.

Geranium Mayburger wanted to know where this whole thing was going to take place and would it be on her street too.

Fleurette Featherstone Fitchell asked all the boys in the seats around her if they wanted to come over and watch it in her back shed.

I said I could stay up and watch it.

Margot Lane said she would stay up and watch it from her bedroom window.

Then Mr. Maynard said a beautiful thing about the moon. He said this: "The lunar surface is fixed and unchanging while the earth changes with each day, month and season. Let a single leaf fall from a tree on earth and there will have been a greater change than may occur on the moon in a hundred autumns."

Mr. Maynard was the best teacher I ever had.

When I got home I thought about Christmas. It was getting close but I didn't have any Christmas feeling yet. I was wondering when it was going to come. You couldn't make it come. It had to just happen.

But it better happen soon, I thought. Time was going on.

After supper at eight o'clock I listened to "Big Town" with Dad while Aunt Dottie put my sister Pamela to bed.

"Big Town" with Steve Wilson of the Illustrated Press and his secretary, the lovely Loreli Kilbourne.

At nine o'clock I got bundled up and went out into the beautiful clear and cold Lowertown winter night and looked up at the full moon.

The shadow of the earth was part way over it, taking a curved bite out of the side.

I could imagine standing there on the moon with this big smooth shadow coming over me. On the moon where nothing ever happens.

One leaf falls, Mr. Maynard said. A big event.

It was so peaceful I started to cry.

The shadow of my earth moved slowly over the smooth moon.

If you looked right at it, you couldn't see it move but if you looked beside it, you could.

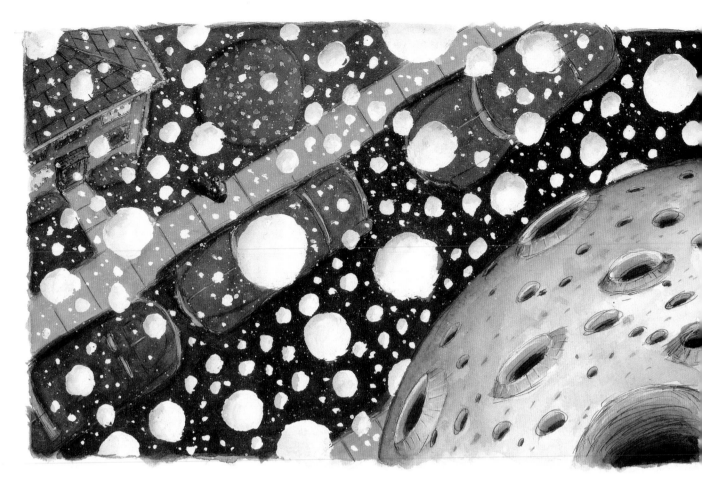

Soon it was completely covered. There was just a furry glow around the outside. Like the frost around my sister's face in her window.

I stood there on Cobourg Street for a while and watched some clouds blow over. I could sniff snow.

Then I could feel the Christmas feeling coming. It was coming over me. Coming up in me. Filling me up.

A feeling of bells and chocolate, hymns and carols, beautiful cold winter and warm rooms. Windows with snow and berries. And laughing and hugging.

In a little while it started to snow.

Big fat flakes.

Every one a big event, Mr. Maynard.

I turned around and went into the house and to bed, letting Christmas come in and out.

❄ ❄ ❄

The next afternoon in Mr. Maynard's class we discussed the eclipse.

Killer Bodnoff said that last night on "Gangbusters" the moon was mentioned. Some crooks were stealing furs from a warehouse and the moon came out and the G-men shot all the crooks in the head.

Arnold Levinson said he was in bed with his eyes shut but he thought he *heard* the eclipse.

Anita Pleet had a huge project already finished, which she presented to Mr. Maynard with pictures pasted on it and printing and arrows explaining the whole thing. She said she read that a day on the moon was 708 hours long.

Martha Banting said, "Mr. Maynard, would you ever be *tired* after a long day like *that, wouldn't* you, Mr. Maynard!" She was so nice.

Geranium Mayburger said she couldn't find the eclipse.

Fleurette Featherstone Fitchell said she was discussing the eclipse in her back shed with some boys and by the time they let her out it was over.

I said that it reminded me of Christmas and then I felt kind of stupid for saying it.

Margot Lane said she watched it from her window and saw the whole thing. She said it made her think of all the other people around Lowertown who were probably watching it too. She said she was imagining what some of the other people in the class were thinking about when they were watching the same thing she was watching.

Or something like that.

Then she looked across the class at me.

At least I thought it was me.

Mr. Maynard had hung up some balsam and spruce and pine branches around the room.

It made the room smell like Christmas. The feeling was getting easy. ❄

VERY LAST FIRST TIME

by JAN ANDREWS   *pictures by* IAN WALLACE

Eva Padlyat lived in a village on Ungava Bay in northern Canada. She was Inuit, and ever since she could remember she had walked with her mother on the bottom of the sea. It was something the people of her village did in winter when they wanted mussels to eat.

Today, something very special was going to happen. Today, for the very first time in her life, Eva would walk on the bottom of the sea alone.

Eva got ready. Standing in their small, warm kitchen, Eva looked at her mother and smiled.

"Shall we go now?"

"I think we'd better."

"We'll start out together, won't we?"

Eva's mother nodded. Pulling up their warm hoods, they went out.

Beside the house there were two sleds, each holding a shovel, a long ice-chisel and a mussel pan. Dragging the sleds behind them, they started off.

Eva and her mother walked through the village. Snow lay white as far as the eye could see—snow, but not a single tree, for miles and miles on the vast northern tundra. The village was off by itself. There were no highways, but snowmobile tracks led away and disappeared into the distance.

Down by the shore they met some friends and stopped for a quick greeting.

They had come at the right time. The tide was out, pulling the sea water away, so there would be room for them to climb under the thick ice and wander about on the seabed.

Eva and her mother walked carefully over the bumps and ridges of the frozen sea. Soon they found a spot where the ice was cracked and broken.

"This is the right place," Eva said.

After shoveling away a pile of snow, she reached for the ice-chisel. She worked it under an ice hump and, heaving and pushing with her mother's help, made a hole.

Eva peered down into the hole and felt the dampness of the air below. She breathed deep to catch the salt sea smell.

"Good luck," Eva's mother said.

Eva grinned. "Good luck yourself."

Her eyes lit up with excitement and she threw her mussel pan into the hole. Then she lowered herself slowly into the darkness, feeling with her feet until they touched a rock and she could let go of the ice above.

In a minute, she was standing on the seabed.

Above her, in the ice hole, the wind whistled. Eva struck a match and lit a candle.

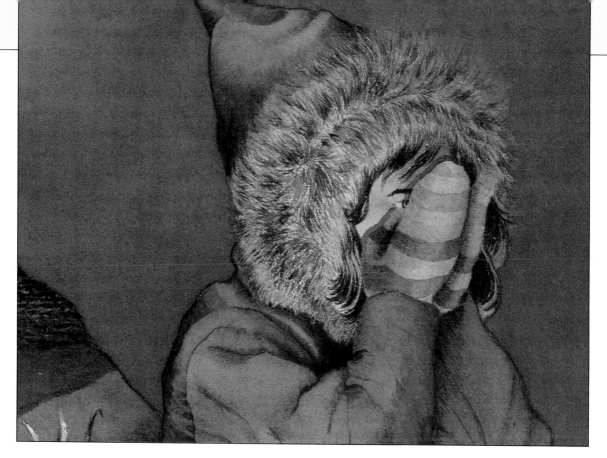

The gold-bright flame shone and glistened on the wet stones and pools at her feet.

She held her candle and saw strange shadow shapes around her. The shadows formed a wolf, a bear, a seal sea-monster. Eva watched them, then she remembered.

"I'd better get to work," she said.

Lighting three more candles, she carefully wedged them between stones so she could see to collect mussels. Using her knife as a lever, she tugged and pried and scraped to pull the mussels off the rocks. She was in luck. There were strings of blue-black mussel shells whichever way she turned.

Alone—for the first time.

Eva was so happy she started to sing. Her song echoed around, so she sang louder. She hummed far back in her throat to make the echoes rumble. She lifted up long strings of mussels and let them clatter into her pan.

Soon her mussel pan was full, so she had time to explore. She found a rock pool that was deep and clear. Small shrimps in the water darted and skittered in the light from her candle. She stopped to watch them. Reaching under a ledge, she touched a pinky-purple crab. The fronds of the anemones on the ledge tickled her wrist.

Beyond the rock pool, seaweed was piled in thick, wet, shiny heaps and masses. Eva scrambled over the seaweed, up and onto a rock mound. Stretching her arms wide, tilting her head back, she laughed, imagining the shifting, waving, lifting swirl of seaweed when the tide comes in.

The tide!

Eva listened. The lap, lap of the waves sounded louder and nearer. Whoosh and roar and whoosh again.

Eva jumped off the rock, stumbled—and her candle dropped and sputtered out. She had gone too far. The candles she had set down between the stones had burned to nothing. There was darkness—darkness all around.

"Help me!" she called, but her voice was swallowed. "Someone come quickly."

Eva closed her eyes. Her hands went to her face. She could not bear to look.

She felt in her pockets. She knew she had more candles there, but she could not seem to find them.

The tide was roaring louder and the ice shrieked and creaked with its movement.

Eva's hands groped deeper. She took a candle out at last and her box of matches, but her fingers were shaking and clumsy. For a long, forever moment, she could not strike the match to light the candle.

The flame seemed pale and weak.

Eva walked slowly, fearfully, peering through the shadows, looking for her mussel pan.

At last, she found it and ran stumbling to the

ice-hole. Then, looking up, Eva saw the moon in the sky. It was high and round and big. Its light cast a circle through the hole onto the seabed at her feet.

Eva stood in the moonlight. Her parka glowed. Blowing out her candle, she slowly began to smile.

By the time her mother came, she was dancing. She was skipping and leaping in and out of the moonglow circle, darkness and light, in and out.

"Eva," her mother called.

"I'm here," she called back. "Take my mussel pan." Eva scrambled onto a rock and held the pan up high to her mother. Then her mother's hands reached down and pulled her up, too, through the hole.

Squeezing her mother's hand, Eva saw the moon, shining on the snow and ice, and felt the wind on her face once more.

"That was my last very first— my very last *first* time—for walking alone on the bottom of the sea," Eva said.

The Island That Took Care of Itself

by SHELLEY TANAKA
pictures by DEBI PERNA

Somewhere in the middle of the ocean, there was a little island. The island looked very bare, covered only by sand. There were no trees. There were no hills or lakes or rivers.

But the island wasn't as empty as it looked. Enough rain and snow fell to fill ponds with fresh water. Between the humps of sand there were green grasses and cranberry bushes for birds to eat. There was even enough grass and water to feed a small herd of wild horses that ran free on the island.

Although there wasn't much on it, the island looked after itself. The horses grew up and had more and more babies, until it looked as though there would not be enough grass to feed them all. But then an extra-cold winter came along. The older and weaker animals died, but their dead bodies rotted and decayed and made the soil rich so the grass could grow well.

The island managed just fine this way for a long, long time.

Then one day, people found the island and decided to move in. They didn't want to eat horses, so they

brought rabbits over on a ship and let them loose. The rabbits had so many babies that soon there were too many for the people to eat. The rabbits ate up the plants and grass, until there was little left for the people or the horses.

So the people brought over cats to eat all the rabbits. The cats did this, but then they started having kittens. Soon there were wild cats all over the island. They were as much of a nuisance as the rabbits. And the people didn't want to eat the cats.

So the people brought over foxes

to eat the cats. But the foxes started to eat the birds, too.

With few birds around to eat them, grasshoppers started to eat up all the plants.

Finally, the people decided enough was enough. They took out their guns and shot all the foxes. Then they packed their bags and went away themselves.

Soon the birds came back and started eating grasshoppers again. The plants grew back. With no rabbits, cats, foxes or people, the island was back to the way it was in the first place.

Once again, it could look after itself.

NIGHT CARS

BY TEDDY JAM

PICTURES BY ERIC BEDDOWS

Once there was a baby
Who wouldn't go to sleep

Tired voices
Walking feet

Passing cars
Noisy street

Night dog watches
Counting all the lights

Night cars gliding
Out of baby's sight

Someone needs a pillow
Call a taxi on the phone

Someone needs a
  goodnight kiss
Someone's eyes have
  fallen down

Baby wakes his father up
Wants to see the night car truck

Slow snow falling deep
Cars dogs babies sleep

Night cars humming
  through the snow
Night cars drifting
Night cars slow

Night cars calling out your
  name
Night cars hiding in your
  dreams

Baby waking up again
Snow has covered everything
White night white dog

Snow plow making
White snow logs

Night cars shining in the
  night
Stop and bow at each red
  light

Engines roar
Light turns green
Night cars on their way
  again

63

Fire engine screams at night
Fire siren fire light

Fire engine fire truck
Waking everybody up

Garbage man garbage man
Careful near that dream

It could gobble up
Your garbage truck
Then where would you be

Night goes
Morning comes

Baby sings
Daddy yawns

Carry those boxes
Slam those doors

Shout those shouts
Fill those stores

Get dressed get washed
    find warm clothes
Thick socks big boots
    kick that snow

Work all night sleep all day
Eat and drink at the Donut
  Café

Chocolate for baby
Coffee for Dad...
...Even night cars go to
  bed.

ROSES SING ON NEW SNOW

A DELICIOUS TALE

Seven days a week, every week of the year, Maylin cooked in her father's restaurant. It was a spot well known throughout the New World for its fine food.

But when compliments and tips were sent to the chef, they never reached Maylin because her father kept the kitchen door closed and told everyone that it was his two sons who did all the cooking.

Maylin's father and brothers were fat and lazy from overeating, for they loved food. Maylin loved food too, but for different reasons. To Chinatown came men lonely and cold and bone-tired. Their families and wives waited in China. But a well-cooked meal would always make them smile. So Maylin worked to renew their spirits and used only the best ingredients in her cooking.

BY PAUL YEE   PICTURES BY HARVEY CHAN

Then one day it was announced that the governor of South China was coming to town. For a special banquet, each restaurant in Chinatown was invited to bring its best dish.

Maylin's father ordered her to spare no expense and to use all her imagination on a new dish. She shopped in the market for fresh fish and knelt in her garden for herbs and greens. In no time she had fashioned a dish of delectable flavors and aromas, which she named Roses Sing on New Snow.

Maylin's father sniffed happily and went off to the banquet, dressed in his best clothes and followed by his two sons.

Now the governor also loved to eat. His eyes lit up like lanterns at the array of platters that arrived. Every kind of meat, every color of vegetable, every bouquet of spices was present. His chopsticks dipped eagerly into every dish.

When he was done, he pointed to Maylin's bowl and said, "That one wins my · warmest praise! It reminded me of China, and yet it transported me far beyond. Tell me, who cooked it?"

Maylin's father waddled forward and repeated the lie he had told so often before. "Your Highness, it was my two sons who prepared it."

"Is that so?" The governor stroked his beard thoughtfully. "Then show my cook how the dish is done. I will present it to my emperor in China and reward you well!"

Maylin's father and brothers rushed home. They burst into the kitchen and forced Maylin to list all her ingredients. Then they made her demonstrate how she had chopped the fish and carved the vegetables and blended the spices. They piled everything into huge baskets and then hurried back.

A stove was set up before the governor and his cook. Maylin's brothers cut the fish and cleaned the vegetables and ground the spices. They stoked a fire and cooked the food. But with one taste, the governor threw down his chopsticks.

"You imposters! Do you take me for a fool?" he bellowed. "That is not Roses Sing on New Snow!"

Maylin's father tiptoed up and peeked. "Why . . . why, there is one spice not here," he stuttered.

"Name it and I will send for it!" roared the impatient governor.

But Maylin's father had no reply, for he knew nothing about spices.

Maylin's older brother took a quick taste and said, "Why, there's one vegetable missing!"

"Name it, and my men will fetch it!" ordered the governor.

But no reply came, for Maylin's older brother knew nothing about food.

Maylin's other brother blamed the fishmonger. "He gave us the wrong kind of fish!" he cried.

"Then name the right one, and my men will fetch it!" said the governor.

Again there was no answer.

Maylin's father and brothers quaked with fear and fell to their knees. When the governor pounded his fist on the chair, the truth quickly spilled out. The guests were astounded to hear that a woman had cooked this dish. Maylin's father hung his head in shame as the governor sent for the real cook.

Maylin strode in and faced the governor and his men. "Your Excellency, you cannot take this dish to China!" she announced.

"What?" cried the governor. "You dare refuse the emperor a chance to taste this wonderful creation?"

"This is a dish of the New World," Maylin said. "You cannot recreate it in the Old."

But the governor ignored her words and scowled. "I can make your father's life miserable here," he threatened her. So she said, "Let you and I cook side by side, so you can see for yourself."

The guests gasped at her daring request. However, the governor nodded, rolled up his sleeves, and donned an apron. Together, Maylin and the governor cut and chopped. Side by side they heated two woks, and then stirred in identical ingredients.

When the two dishes were finally finished, the governor took a taste from both. His face paled, for they were different.

"What is your secret?" he demanded. "We selected the same ingredients and cooked side by side!"

"If you and I sat down with paper and brush and black ink, could we bring forth identical paintings?" asked Maylin.

From that day on Maylin was renowned in Chinatown as a great cook and a wise person. Her fame even reached as far as China.

But the emperor, despite the governor's best efforts, was never able to taste that most delicious New World dish, nor to hear Roses Sing on New Snow.

from MORRIS RUMPEL AND THE WINGS OF ICARUS

BY **Betty Waterton**   PICTURES BY **Keith Lee**

"Here's your seat, Morris, right beside the window," said the stewardess. "Enjoy your flight to Cranberry Corners!"

"You know all about me!" Morris looked at her in surprise. *Wow!* he thought. *Are you ever beautiful!*

The stewardess smiled a dazzling smile. "We have to know about our special passengers," she said, stowing his backpack and the nasturtiums in the overhead compartment. "My goodness, this pack is really heavy!"

"Not for me. I've been working on my biceps lately." Morris flexed his arm to show her. He was just about to tell her about his body-building program, when a large lady with a knitting bag sat down beside him.

"I'll be seeing you later, Morris," said the stewardess. As she retreated before the swarm of advancing passengers, she winked.

Morris blinked back.

In case such an opportunity arose again, he began to practise winking. But each time he tried it, he could see his nose twitch out of the corner of his eye, and feel his mouth open.

The large lady took some knitting out of her bag and began to knit on an afghan. As she knit, she gazed around her contentedly. Suddenly she noticed Morris's twitching face. "Are you all right, dear?" she asked. "Shall I call the attendant?"

"No, thanks," mumbled Morris. "I'm okay." Then he turned his face to the window and intently studied the top of the wing.

Feeling a little pang in his stomach, he remembered Quincy's chocolate bar. He pulled it out of his pocket and peeled back the paper. The chocolate was melting, so he ate it quickly. Then he opened Leah's horse magazine to an interesting-looking picture of some large worms. The article was called "How to Worm Your Pony." It was not as interesting as the picture.

The stewardess's voice came crackling through the plane. "Please make sure your seatbelts are fastened, in preparation for takeoff!" *She sounds different on the intercom*, thought Morris. *More like my teacher!*

Click! Click! Click! All around him, people were clicking on their seatbelts. Groping frantically, Morris hunted, but he could only find one end of his. Suddenly he was filled with panic. He held up his arm and waved it.

"I haven't got one!" he cried.

The beautiful stewardess hurried down the aisle to help him, and the missing strap was quickly located. Morris had been sitting on it.

As the plane taxied to the runway, Morris turned his attention to the takeoff. The motors revved, and the plane surged forward. *It's just like being in a Ferrari!* he thought, as they roared past the airport buildings.

Then all at once they were airborne and climbing. Morris's stomach went tight with excitement.

He stared out the window. Below him were little Monopoly houses and cars like Dinky toys. He couldn't tell which were trees and which were just bushes. They all looked the same from above! For a while he puzzled over tiny rectangles and ovals that shimmered like jewels in some back-yards, until he realized they must be swimming pools. They got smaller and smaller. Finally he couldn't make them out at all. The plane levelled off, and everything got quiet.

Maybe this is what I'll do for the rest of my life, he thought as they cruised among the clouds. *Fly!*

Now, through breaks in the clouds, he could see the mountain peaks. Some still had snow on them.

Far below, he could see moving specks. Birds! He was flying above the birds!

No wonder Grandpa Rumpel is always talking about his flying days!

The plane droned on. The afghan lady fell asleep. Other people were reading or talking. The man in the seat in front of him was looking out the window through binoculars.

Then Morris discovered the aircraft safety manual in the pocket of the seat ahead. He was delighted to find it had all kinds of information about the plane—how to put on your life jacket, where the emergency exits were and, best of all, how to use your oxygen mask. *Totally excellent!* thought Morris. *I wonder if it's free?*

The more he thought about it, the more he wanted the manual. But what if he wasn't supposed to take it? He glanced carefully around. Beside him, the afghan lady was dozing, her knitting in a heap on her lap.

With one quick movement, Morris slipped the manual between the pages of Leah's horse magazine. Then, turning his face to the window, he pretended to study the clouds.

Suddenly he heard a voice. "Come with me, Morris. The captain would like to talk to you!"

Morris jumped. Looking up, he saw the beautiful stewardess. She was standing in the aisle, wiggling her finger at him.

"Me?" he croaked. She nodded.

Had she seen him hiding the aircraft manual? What was going to happen to him now? What would his grandparents say if they heard about this? Worse, what would his parents say?

"I don't...uh...think I can get out," mumbled Morris.

"Of course you can, dear!" said the afghan lady. Now fully awake, she rose ponderously and stood in the aisle.

The stewardess was smiling her dazzling smile. The other passengers were smiling. *Nobody knows*, thought Morris. *Nobody knows I'm ripping off the airline!*

There was only one thing to do. As he sidled out, he slid Leah's magazine with its incriminating evidence deep into the seat pocket. Then, breathing a sigh of relief, he followed the stewardess to the front of the plane.

As he stepped into the cockpit, the pilot and co-pilot turned and smiled at him. Morris grinned back.

"Oh, boy!" he said. "What a beautiful instrument panel! Look! There's something up in the corner of your weather radar screen."

"That's right, son. There's a thunderstorm

disturbance off to the left. But it's too far away to bother us on this flight. I see you know something about planes."

Morris blushed. "Sometimes I read Grandpa Rumpel's flying magazines. He used to be a Spitfire pilot. I might be a pilot, too, some day, because I've probably got some of his genes."

"Well, good luck, boy. Enjoy the rest of the flight!"

"I sure will!"

Smiling proudly, Morris returned to his seat. "Well," said the afghan lady. "How did you like the cockpit?"

"It was awesome! My Grandpa Rumpel is a pilot, too, you know."

"Does he still fly?"

"Not anymore. He and Grandma have a ranch beside Cranberry lake, and I'm going there for a holiday. It'll be cool, because they've got all kinds of wild animals around there!"

"Like moose and bear, I suppose."

"Well, more like deer and stuff. And hawks. Grandpa says this year they've got some very special hawks nesting near Rumpel Ranch. But it's kind of a secret."

At that moment the flight attendants began serving trays of food, and Morris forgot about everything else. "Let the good times roll!" he cried, eagerly opening his first little plastic container.

It held a small chicken salad and a big pickle. There was also a bun and a piece of carrot cake, and a Coke. Morris quickly ate it all. Luckily, the afghan lady wasn't hungry, so he ate hers as well.

"How did you enjoy your light snack?" asked the stewardess when she came to collect the trays.

"It certainly was light," said Morris. ✛

THE HOUR

By Tim Wynne-Jones

It is night. Fred and Dreadnought are asleep. Mum and Dad are asleep. Thunder and Frisco and Lyle are asleep. But not me.

It is the Hour of the Frog.

What's that? Drip. Drip. Drip.

Thlump! Out of his slimy hole in the wall . . . Thlump. Thlump. Thlump.

He crosses the living room floor. Thlippety-thlump. Thlippety-thlump. Thlippety-thlop-thlop. Thlippety-thlump, to dance in his frog suit up and down the front hall. Then off to the kitchen.

THE FROG

What's that? The knife in the pickle jar. Frog
is making a sandwich. Eggs and mayo, peanut
butter, onions and
Flies! On a sticky
bun. The Hour of
the Frog snack.

Pictures by Catharine O'Neill

Thlump. Slurp. Bump. He's heading my way.
I pull the covers up over my head. Thlump.
Thlump. He's at the foot of the stairs. The smell
of pickle juice floats up in the air and through my
open door. Thlump. Bump. Burp. Slurp. Bump.

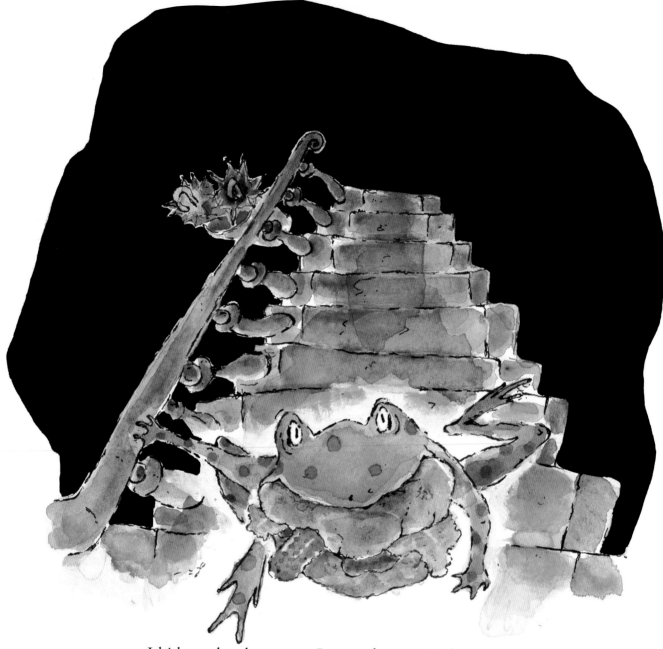

I hide under the covers. I try to keep quiet but . . .
Thlump. Bump.

I can't stop myself. "Oh no," says I. "Oh woe is me."

And there in the gloom of the landing Frog stops in his
slimy tracks. "Oh, woe?" says he. "Ho, ho," says he. "You
don't scare me."

"Oh no?" says I, rising way up high. Then "Go!" I cry.
And Froggy leaps almost out of his skin onto the banister.

Then thlippety-thlump. I hear
Frog jump a-wooing all the way back
to his slimy hole in the wall. Back to
the swamp. SPLAASH! Like every
night.

But I still can't sleep. So I turn my
mind to breakfast. French toast and
butter . . . Zzz . . . Maple syrup . . . and
. . . Flies!

CONTRIBUTORS

Groundwood Books is proud to work with many exceptional authors and gifted illustrators. Admired and loved throughout Canada, these authors and illustrators have helped to make Canada an internationally recognized leader in children's book publishing. For complete lists of their books available from Groundwood, write to the publisher at the address on the copyright page.

Storyteller **Jan Andrews** is renowned in Canada and abroad for her outstanding picture book texts, among them *Very Last First Time*, *The Auction*, and *Pumpkin Time*. Jan lives near Ottawa and is at work on her first novel, *Keri*, to be published in 1996.

Eric Beddows is famous as the illustrator of the award-winning Zoom books which have been published in many countries. He has also illustrated other well-loved children's books including *Night Cars*. A fine artist who exhibits under the name Ken Nutt, Eric lives in Stratford, Ontario.

Steve Beinicke, one of Canada's best multi-media creators, makes exciting CD-ROMs. Despite his mastery of advanced technology, Steve still loves illustrating picture books and non-fiction for children, as well as painting. He lives in Toronto.

John Bianchi, best known today as the author and illustrator of the Bungalo Boys books, started out drawing pictures for other authors' books. The first picture book he illustrated, *The Dingles* by Helen Levchuk, was turned into an animated film by the National Film Board and nominated for a Genie award. John lives in Tucson, Arizona.

Ever since **Ann Blades** wrote and illustrated *Mary of Mile 18*, she has been one of the country's finest and most popular illustrators. She also illustrated Betty Waterton's *A Salmon for Simon* which won several major awards when it was published and later became a Canadian classic. Ann lives in White Rock, British Columbia.

Born and raised in Hong Kong, **Harvey Chan** is one of the most talented and versatile young illustrators to appear on the scene in the past few years. Now living in Toronto, Harvey uses his end-lessly inventive skill to create illustrations that are uniquely suited to each book he works on.

"Off the wall", "hilarious", and "crazy" are words often used to describe the work of **Gary Clement**. Well-known as a magazine illustrator, he brings a breath of fresh air to children's books with his original talent. Gary is now writing his own stories as well: he is the author of *Just Stay Put* which he also illustrated. He lives in Toronto.

Hey Dad!, **Brian Doyle**'s first novel, changed the course of Canadian publishing for young readers. His fresh innovative approach to storytelling and his use of language were originally considered shocking. Now Brian is Canada's best-loved young people's novelist with many award-winning books to his credit. Brian lives in Ottawa, where almost all his books are set.

Joanne Fitzgerald is an illustrator whose pictures evoke an instant positive response: no one is better at creating cozy, charming, yet original worlds and characters. Joanne is currently working on a companion to *Doctor Kiss Says Yes* called *Jacob's Best Sisters*. She lives in Georgetown, Ontario.

Who is the mysterious **Teddy Jam**? Some people believe that Teddy, who sometimes claims to be a hairdresser from Owen Sound, is an author for adults in his/her other life. Author of such well-known books as *Year of Fire* and the award-winning *Doctor Kiss Says Yes*, Teddy Jam—whoever he/she may be—really knows how a child's mind works. No one knows where Teddy lives.

Kim LaFave had done a lot of work in advertising before illustrating *Amos's Sweater* in 1988. It has become one of the best-selling picture books in Canada. Kim now lives on the Sunshine Coast of British Columbia where he is a publisher in his own right.

Day Songs Night Songs is **Keith Lee**'s first picture book. He came to Canada from Hong Kong where he was the art director for a popular children's magazine. A resident of Toronto, Keith hopes that one day soon he will make a full-time living as a picture book illustrator.

Just like her fictional character Doris Dingle, **Helen Levchuk** loves her cats and her garden. Helen realized the dream of many aspiring writers when her unsolicited manuscript for *The Dingles* was accepted and published by Groundwood Books. She lives in Niagara-on-the-Lake, Ontario.

One of the best-known names in Canadian children's books, **Janet Lunn** is famous for her award-winning novels, non-fiction, and picture book texts. After many years between picture books, Janet will have a new story published in the near future. She lives in Prince Edward County, Ontario.

Catharine O'Neill has produced three books for children, two of which she wrote as well as illustrated and each one highly original and witty. A resident of Ithaca, New York, Catharine is slowly but surely at work on her next book.

Known to children across the country for her work in *Chickadee* Magazine, **Debi Perna** is also a book illustrator whose gentle, evocative style is well-suited to texts for very young children. Debi lives in Toronto.

A poet and children's novelist, **Robert Priest** is also a rock-and-roller and children's musician. He lives in Toronto where he performs and records with his band "The Teds."

Niko Scharer writes books when she isn't completing her PhD in philosophy. Her first book, *Emily's House* which she wrote when she was still an undergraduate, was a best-seller in North America. Niko lives in Toronto.

Ulli Steltzer is an eminent photographer whose books on the Inuit of Canada's Arctic and the aboriginal peoples of British Columbia, Guatemala, and other places have won her a worldwide reputation. Ulli lives in Vancouver.

Shelley Tanaka is both an author and an editor with countless adult and children's books to her credit. She lives in a beautiful farmhouse in rural Ontario.

Ian Wallace has established an international reputation as one of Canada's most creative and boldly experimental illustrators and is a recent Canadian nominee for the illustrious Hans Christian Andersen Award given by the International Board on Books for Young People. Ian's next book, *Sarah and the People of Sand River*, will be published in 1996. He lives in Toronto.

Betty Waterton is the author of such classics as *A Salmon for Simon* and *Pettranella* as well as the creator of the wacky Quincy Rumpel novels for young readers. Betty lives on Vancouver Island, British Columbia.

A man of many talents, **Tim Wynne-Jones** is the author of adult fiction, children's novels, and picture books as well as a book designer, publisher, and musician. His multi-award-winning collection of short stories, *Some of the Kinder Planets*, most recently won the prestigious Boston Globe-Horn Book Award. Tim lives in Perth, Ontario.

Paul Yee, whose family came to Canada in the first wave of Chinese migration at the turn of the century, has dedicated his writing life to commemorating the stories of those who helped to build this country in the face of racism and discrimination. His *Tales from Gold Mountain* was an international success. Paul lives in Toronto.

Index

Franklin Pierce College Library

00150087

DATE DUE